THE
MENEHUNE

Don W. Hill, M.D.

ISBN 978-1-969268-19-9 (paperback)
ISBN 978-1-969268-20-5 (hardcover)
ISBN 978-1-969268-18-2 (digital)

Some characters and events in this book are fictitious and products of the author's imagination. Any similarity to real persons, living or dead, is coincidental and not intended by the author.

Printed in the United States of America

DON W HILL
PUBLISHING

INTRODUCTION

This work of fiction was inspired by a documented post-WWII historical event. As records indicate, a school superintendent named, George London, and his students had a first-hand encounter with a potentially hostile band of stone-age warriors in the Waimea Valley, deep in the dense jungles of northern Oahu, Hawaii. This tribe was thought to be a remnant of the lost race of a prehistoric people known as, the Menehune. Well, could the Menehune still exist? Although the events concerning the Waimea Valley sighting occurred years ago in the 1940s, it certainly should still give one pause to wonder…

DEDICATION

To Susan Carol Maple:
If it wasn't for you, I would have never lived in Hawaii years
ago, and this story would have never come to fruition!

CHAPTER 1

HISTORICAL (AND HUMAN) RELICS

La Paloma Del Pacifico was clearly the most diminutive cruise ship in the more modern times of the late 20th century to ever slip through the sapphire-blue ocean waters that caressed the famed golden beaches of the Hawaiian archipelago. Despite its truncated over-all length and beam, it was nonetheless touted to be the most luxurious vessel afloat at that particular time in seafaring history. Perhaps this self-ascribed mantle of opulent excellence was merely a *subjective* attribute, adopted for purely promotional commercial intent.

On the other hand, maybe the veracity of this acclamation was truly an *objective* phenomenon. In all likelihood, it was an amalgamation of two opposing perspectives in an overlapping universe of distinct possibilities. After all, this vaunted inter-island pleasure cruiser was fully booked out for thirteen months or more in advance, with a waiting list to board that was, figuratively speaking, a nautical mile long. Did that indisputable fact alone not speak volumes?

Constructed at great expense in port city of Bremerhaven at the Meeresarbeiten GmbH shipyards in northern West Germany, the keel was laid in the spring of 1983. The vessel was originally commissioned by the Transpacifico Consortium and it flew under the flag of Mexico. Despite its Latino affiliation, the entire crew, to the very last man, came from the other four corners of the Earth. The cabin stewards, deck workers, custodians, and kitchen crew hailed predominantly from the Philippines, Malaysia, equatorial Africa, and the greater Indian sub-continent in that particular order. The engineers, maintenance staff, and ship officers, on the other hand, were all from central or northern Europe, and that included the commander of the vessel, Captain Nils Skarsgard.

La Paloma Del Pacifico would depart from its berth in Honolulu each Sunday evening and set out on a seven day pleasure cruise with scheduled visits at the Port of Kahului in Maui followed by a trip south to the relatively arid, west side of the Big Island to visit Kona. The ship would then circumnavigate the southern aspect of the Big Island on the following day and allow its passengers to depart for a day excursion at the lush and tropical port of Hilo before departing and turning north to make a stop at the harbor in Lihue on the Garden Isle of Kauai. Finally returning to Honolulu upon the terminus of the cruise on the following Saturday, the passengers would depart with hopefully, a lifetime of romantic and happy memories.

This idyllic itinerary had to be radically altered after Hurricane Iniki slammed into the island of Kauai on September 5, 1992. This violent tropical storm was the most powerful hurricane to ever strike the Hawaiian Island chain in recorded human history, inflicting over three billion dollars-worth of property damage in addition to numerous casualties. Following a one-month moratorium after the vicious assault inflicted by Hurricane Iniki, the financially avaricious and morally agnostic cruise ship industry prematurely resumed tourist visitations to the island of Kauai by mid-October of 1992.

As one might predict, this rush to return to commerce-as-usual would end up being little more than an unmitigated public relations failure. By the time the tourists had finally returned to Kauai only one month after the land-fall of Iniki, very little reparative recovery efforts to manage the disaster had been undertaken. Visitors had been greeted by the horrific visage of flattened homes, up-rooted ancient trees, and districts on the island that still lacked running water, electrical power, or an operative sewage system.

When *La Paloma Del Pacifico* returned to its home port in Honolulu on October 15, 1992, it would turn out to be the very first time that the majority of the passengers on this particular cruise ship would give the voyage an overall negative rating on their collective vacation experience. This was all a consequence to the port of call made to Lihue, Kauai, which was initiated only one month after the Iniki hurricane land-fall.

Although the corporate bean-counters at the Transpacifico Consortium apparently had "put the cart in front of the horse" on this latest inter-island cruise, it would not be a mistake that they would likely make again. Sadly, it would be a long time before *La Paloma Del Pacifico* would ever pay another port-of-call visit to the Island of Kauai, as the citizens of the Garden Isle were faced with months, and perhaps even years, of restorative remediation. On the next inter-island voyage, Transpacifico had to reformulate the itinerary of their flagship, and time was of the essence.

On the following inter-island cruise which was slated to set sail on Sunday, October 17, 1992, Captain Nils Skarsgard charted a new plan to spend an additional day on the island of Maui and avoid going to the island of Kauai altogether. One full day would be spent in the port city of Kahului, and then the ship would cruise around the western aspect of Maui between Molokai and Lanai to make a port-of-call on the south end of the Maui valley isthmus at the small port village of Maalaea. The only issue was that *La Paloma Del Pacifico* would have to drop anchor a few hundred yards south of the port village, and any passengers who wanted to go ashore to enjoy an excursion would have to be ferried back and forth by one of the ship's tender boats.

For Captain Skarsgard and his crew, this turned out to be a good plan. A minor mutiny had brewed amongst some of the affluent passengers when it was learned that the ship would not be making a trip to Kauai as originally planned, but any dissention was quickly quelled when the captain declared that an open-bar, ad-lib, no-limit, alcohol consumption grant would be cheerfully bestowed au gratis upon all of the passengers for the duration of the cruise.

On the evening when *La Paloma Del Pacifico* finally hoisted its anchor to set sail from Maalaea, it navigated toward its new destination which was Kona, on the Big Island. The cruise ship motored past the eastern aspect of the island of Kahoolawe. The island, at nearly 45 square miles, was the eighth largest island in the Hawaiian chain, and could be readily found only seven miles south of the island of Maui..

Previously utilized as a penal colony by the Hawaiian Kingdom in the remote past, there were no longer any residents on the desert island of Kahoolawe in modern times. This was predominantly a consequence to the lack of any appreciable potable water. The other issue was that the unoccupied island had been used exclusively as a target practice range for the United States Navy for half a century, dating all the way back to WWII.

A subsequent prolonged and vehement protest from the citizens of Hawaii finally ended the incessant and merciless bombardment of Kahoolawe only two years earlier, back in 1990. Unfortunately, an incalculable amount of unexploded ordnance left the island a contaminated and dangerous place to visit, and the federal government issued a decree at that time that no visitors should ever set foot upon that wrecked piece of volcanic real estate. That's why the look-out on the bridge was alarmed to witness through his binoculars what appeared to be an abandoned thirty-two foot, twin-powered catamaran rolling about gently in the surf about forty yards from the rocky Kahoolawe coast line.

Nils Skarsgard at the time was hosting the black-tie/formal gown Captain's Reception Night in the main lounge, and he generally did not like to be disturbed when he was attending one of these opulent and mandatory functions, unless it was of course an emergency. Well, this situation appeared to be an emergency. The second in command had sent a radio communique to the Coast Guard post back in Maalaea Harbor, but the cutter was indisposed on an illegal drug shipment interdiction mission on western Maui, and it could not immediately respond to the situation. It appeared that the malicious Chi-coms were attempting to yet again flood the islands with tons of illicit recreational drugs. That matter, at least in the opinion of the U.S. Coast Guard, seemed to have a higher priority.

When the captain was called to the bridge, the second in command and look-out watchman filled out what little was known about the situation to Nils Skarsgard.

"The Coast Guard believes that this abandoned vessel off the Kahoolawe coast might be *The Poly-Tech Princess* that disappeared over two weeks ago," the second officer explained. "I was informed that the boat was a research catamaran owned by the Polynesian Pacific Research Institute. A party of five individuals went to explore an anomaly that was captured in a photograph taken by a satellite from outer space. The crew, and *The Poly-Tech Princess*, at least up until now, had simply disappeared."

"What kind of anomaly were they looking for?" Captain Skarsgard asked.

"Can't rightly say," the second officer reported, "however, based upon the satellite photo, there was apparently a sea vessel of political, historical, or military importance that was found partially imbedded in the ancient, rocky, Waikono dry river bed in East Maui. Whatever they found is believed to date back perhaps as far as WWII!"

"West of Kaupo?!" Skargard asked. "Why hell, son! There's nothing out there but the remnants of the old, burned out St. Isaac's Orthodox Church that was originally built around 1817 by the Russian colony that somehow mysteriously disappeared back then."

Turning to the look-out, Skarsgard pressed for more information. "What can you tell me about the craft that you visualized through your binoculars?"

"It fits the bill, Cap. The port side boat railing of the catamaran is clearly mangled, but no sign of life, however," the look-out reported. "From my vantage point on our deck, I had a straight shot to peer down into the hold of that vessel. No bodies, living or otherwise. The Coast Guard wants us to launch one of our tender boats and tow it back to Maalaea where they'll meet us there with a team of experts. In case foul play had occurred and the vessel turns out to be a crime scene, they don't want any of our crew members to board the catamaran. We've been ordered only to draw a tow rope through the bow eye, secure it, and then haul the damned thing back to port. They want it done, and they want it done *now*! No 'ifs, ands or buts' about the matter, and that's their final word."

"Get it done," the Captain ordered the second officer after a stifled sigh of resignation. "Find a berth for the tender in Maalaea and then simply kick back and relax for a few days once you tow that catamaran carcass back to the Coast Guard. We'll reel you back in a week from now when *La Paloma Del Pacifico* comes back through during her next voyage."

"What do you make of this situation, Captain?" the bridge look-out asked.

"Sadly, people do indeed seem to inexplicably disappear in these islands at intermittent intervals, and for no apparent reason," Skarsgard answered. "It's as if the missing get swallowed up whole. Out here, there's no telling what kind of evil shit that a human being might stumble into from time to time."

"Truly odd," the bridge lookout concluded.

"Be that as it may," Captain Skarsgard pondered, "I wonder why the Coast Guard has a bug up its back-side over what seems to me to be a rather trivial matter?"

"Maybe," the second officer interjected with a cautionary pause, "it has something to do with the simple fact that, for unclear reasons, an FBI agent and a politico from the State Department were assigned to be crew members on that catamaran. Now, they're amongst the missing!"

Over two weeks earlier, on Saturday, October 2, 1992, Professor Grover Ali'i from the Polynesian Pacific Research Institute was patiently waiting at the Kahului Airport for the arrival of three individuals from the mainland who were commissioned to accompany him on a field trip to eastern Maui to investigate the sudden appearance of an anomaly of potentially important historical significance. When Hurricane Iniki hit the Hawaiian Islands a month earlier, the brunt of the damage was done to the northern island of Kauai. Thankfully, the hurricane had only brushed by Maui, causing some coastal erosion. A severe wash-out of the St. Isaac's Church Road occurred, however. This old, narrow, unpaved dirt road west of Kaupo, peeled toward the shoreline, directly off the Piiliani Highway, which incidentally, was also noted to receive a minor, sub-lethal erosion injury from the storm.

Professor Ali'i chuckled at the nomenclature bestowed upon the Piiliani Highway, as frankly, it was little more than another rutted dirt road that ran through the hinterlands of the remote Kaupo district. In any event, the coastal erosion that was a consequence to the battering waves engendered as a consequence to the passing hurricane had partially exposed some type of a peculiar, rusty, cigar-shaped, metallic object that had been previously buried under the river rocks at the mouth of the Waikono dry river bed. Whatever the object was, it warranted a scientific investigation.

The mouth of the dead Waikono River was eighty-five feet wide, but who knows how long ago in the remote past that any meaningful volume of water had flowed over the river bed? Reportedly, there was at one time water in the Waikono when the Russian settlers came in the early 1800s. Upon a small, eroded volcanic cinder cone immediately to the west and adjacent to the mouth of the river bed, were the remnants of St. Isaac's Orthodox Church.

The Russians came to Hawaii and built Fort Elizavety (Elizabeth) in the Waimea district on Kauai in 1817, and subsequently attempted to establish a colony near the mouth of the Waikono River in eastern Maui. Little is known of the fate of the Russian settlers. The colony had apparently thrived for about three years or so before the inhabitants, including every man, woman, and child, had mysteriously vanished into thin air without leaving any trace. Afterward, their beloved lava rock and wooden Christian church was violently razed to the ground.

Grover Ali'i was an anthropologist by training, and was therefore well-versed with the history of the human inhabitants of the Hawaiian Islands. He had long-studied the history of the Russian colonists in Hawaii, and he had formulated an unsubstantiated opinion that the Russians must have seriously pissed-off somebody along the way, and the Slavic immigrants were all eventually ambushed and violently slaughtered to the last settler.

As no trace was ever found, Professor Ali'i had formulated the rather unorthodox opinion that the Caucasian colonists had been *cannibalized*! Now, the Polynesians didn't routinely practice cannibalism per se, but the Fijians certainly did up until the mid-1800s, and these individuals were members of a completely different ethnic group than their Polynesian neighbors. The Fijians, after all, were *Melanesians*. It certainly gave one pause to wonder.

Could there have been at one time or another a separate group of humans that dwelled in parallel proximity to the Polynesians on the Hawaiian Islands who could have perpetrated such a foul deed upon the hapless Russian colonists? Well, of course. One should never underestimate the savage brutality that one band of human beings can unleash upon some other, unrelated tribal group who are believed to look, talk, or think differently than themselves. Humans are sadly hard-wired to behave in such a tribal, "we vs. them", merciless fashion. How else can historical acts of genocide be otherwise explained?

Be that as it may, one issue concerning the good professor's participation on this scientific quest remained to be answered. Dr. Ali'i was, after all, an *anthropologist*. He was not an archeologist or historian per se. It was certainly unclear as to why a scientist in his particular field of expertise would be needed on this type of expedition to investigate some rusty, metallic artifact of unknown significance. Nonetheless, his involvement in the project was not through a polite request or invitation. The edict that had been issued to him by the State Department was actually a rather blunt order that he could not readily refuse.

Well, for Professor Ali'i, that was more than enough time for pointless ruminations about the minor tribal foibles that had adversely affected the human condition for eons. It was now time for Professor Ali'i to meet the three individuals who were to accompany him on the expedition. He met them in the baggage claim area, and he readily recognized the trio, as they were all wearing their pre-travel, agreed-upon, red baseball caps with an American flag emblazoned across the bill.

One of the individuals was a tall and rugged appearing Caucasian male with a coarse, jet black man-doo, sporting "white-walls" above the ears and a perfectly plastered coif held into place with what was likely a liberal application of hair gel. The other two people that had accompanied this distinguished appearing gentleman were both women. One was a trim, blonde haired lady who clearly appeared to be a bit on the thin side, yet was nonetheless strikingly attractive. The third person who rounded out the trio was a no-nonsense, physically fit appearing middle-age black woman with a short-cropped reddish tinged Afro.

All three of the professor's new team members were decked out in jogging suits, which in the early nineties, would have been readily considered by many to be haute couture ensembles during the heady, yet waning days of the first Bush administration. Nonetheless, although the ocular features of all three travelers were hidden behind fashionable dark sunglasses. The three individuals maintained a stern and somewhat inflexible continence, indicating they were collectively ready to get down to some serious business.

"Hello, everybody," Professor Ali'i said with a wave as he proceeded to greet his new companions with a customary hand shake.

"Allow me to introduce not only myself, but also my two colleagues," the tall man replied. "My name is special agent, Jeb McClellan with the FBI. The young woman with blonde hair standing to your right is Tricia Portal from the State Department. She's the go-to administrator when it comes to Japanese/American political affairs."

"Charmed, I'm sure," Tricia said as she forcefully grasped the right hand of Professor Ali'i in an unveiled attempt to establish an "alpha-dog" political dominance over the host of the expedition.

"In all likelihood, the most important person rounding out this intrepid band of explorers who is standing to what would be your immediate left, is none-other than Lieutenant, JG rank, Dr. Mabel Harris," McClellan stated. "She's our expert on WWII-era, Japanese and German naval weaponry platforms."

"Correction," the black woman interjected. "I'm now retired from the military. I used to have a teaching post at the Academy, but I was put out to pasture at the twenty year mark. I now teach master-level classes in U.S. History at my current digs which would be the New Iberia Christian College in Louisiana."

"Do you have a PhD?" Ali'i asked.

"I do indeed," Mabel Harris responded. "I published a ground-breaking thesis on the Japanese Imperial Navy's WWII, F-GO atomic bomb project under the direction of Professor Bunsaku Arakatsu at the Kyoto Imperial University."

"Wow! I'm impressed," Ali'i interjected. "For my own edification, how close did the Japanese get to the finish line on their own bomb project?"

"It took a lot of data mining on site at Kyoto, but from what I discovered on my part at the very end, well–" Professor Harris paused as she pursed her lips and slowly shook her head. "I guess you really don't want to know…"

"Good grief! How on Earth were you able to accomplish this kind of research in Japan to complete your doctoral thesis?" Tricia Portal asked.

"I'm fluent in Japanese," Harris answered smugly. "Aren't you? After all, you're supposed to be the point-man, or woman as the case may, on Japanese/American political affairs for this current administration, are you not?"

With a furrowed brow, Tricia Portal could only stare at Mabel Harris without verbally responding.

"Tell me, Dr. Ali'i," Professor Harris queried, "how are we getting to the site where the rusty, tube-shaped anomaly was discovered on the Waikono river bed via satellite photos? I assume you'll be driving us out there?"

"Fat chance," Grover Ali'i responded as he picked up two duffle bags that were traversing upon the luggage carousel, respectively belonging to Tricia Portal and Professor Mabel Harris. "We'll have to go by boat and cruise to the site by skirting along the southern aspect of Maui. I have my private vehicle here at the airport, and I'll drive us all down to the Maalaea Harbor where Skipper Norman Nishioka is waiting there for us with the Polynesian Pacific Research Institute's very own, thirty-two foot, twin-powered cat named, *The Poly-Tech Princess.*"

"Damn!" Tricia Portal exclaimed. "I find the ocean to be somewhat, well-intimidating. Are you sure we can't get their by car?"

"Although Highway 31, also called the Piilani Highway, is now open if one truly desires the opportunity to circumnavigate the entire island, the St. Isaac's Church Road was washed out by Hurricane Iniki last month," Professor Ali'i explained.

"Although it can be easily found on the tax maps as an officially designated County of Maui chartered road way, I heard on the news that the Federal Highway Administration has, for some strange reason, taken a peculiar interest in the repair of this simple one-lane dirt road, of late. The feds apparently brought in a bulldozer and road grader, but these mechanical monsters were only on site for just one day before the project was shut down for unclear reasons. It's all very strange, if you ask me! Nonetheless, I anticipate that the much-needed road repair work will at some point get finished eventually, however."

"No!" Agent McClellan sharply interjected as the party of four walked toward the exit, "If the truth be told, the St. Isaac's Church Road will *never* get repaired at this point in time. Not now, not ever. The county decommissioned the road and the scheduled repair work was subsequently abandoned. Did you know that? According to state law, if a county road is abandoned, the State of Hawaii has the legal option to assume stewardship of the road. When the state of Hawaii rejected this viable option, the road fell under the jurisdiction of the United States Department of the Interior. Uncle Sam changed his rather fickle mind, and instead of fixing the damned dirt road, it now wants to make it absolutely certain that this road will never be utilized again in the future for *any* reason."

"What on earth are you talking about?" Dr. Ali'i asked as he unlocked his car doors to give his traveling companions an opportunity to enter the sedan. "There is, or shall I say, there was an important historical archeological site near the mouth of the Waikono dry river bed. That was the location of the original Saint Isaac's Orthodox Church which was built by the lost Russian colony. Besides, I know for a fact that the road, at least at one time, was also utilized to gain access to the privately owned Akina family cattle ranch near the coast."

"Not anymore," special agent McClellan answered. "The entire Akina family has mysteriously disappeared."

"Wait—just like the Russian colony disappeared back in the early 1800s?!" Grover Ali'i asked with a timbre of alarm resonating from his vocal cords.

"That appears to be the case," McClellan answered with a shrug.

"Does anybody even give two shits about this peculiar circum-stance? Don't you find this whole current situation, well— a bit odd?" Ali'i pressed.

"Not if you have access to the same dossier about this matter that I do," the agent answered in an aloof and nonchalant manner. "In any event, when the Akina family disappeared, the estate fell into arrears on taxes that were owed to the government, now dating back for several years. One man's loss is another man's, well– what can I say? You know the rest. Too bad, so sad. As misfortune of one type or another befell the Akina clan, the entire ranch now belongs to Uncle Sam. The government laid claim to the entire eighty acre estate in July of this year, about two months before Hurricane Iniki paid a most unwelcome visit to this little tropical paradise called, Hawaii."

"What?!" Dr. Ali'i asked in utter astonishment as he turned his head to the right to look at the man who was sitting directly next to him in the passenger seat of the sedan. "Who in hell are you?"

"You already know my name, professor" the agent answered as he issued an unmistakable hostile glare in the direction of Grover Ali'i.

"What could a gumshoe like you possibly offer this research team that's now on an expedition to find what I presume to be a WWII historical relic of Japanese origin? Nobody has out-right said jack-shit to me as to what we're looking for, but I have a good idea from what I've heard thus far."

"Do you, now?" McClellan scoffed.

"After all, one member of this team is a State Department liaison official with expertise in Japanese/American affairs, and the other is an expert on the naval weapons that were utilized by the Axis powers during WWII. Am I getting warm yet?" Ali'i asked while Dr. Mabel Harris and Ms. Trisha Portal smiled and sheepishly waved from the back seat of the sedan after it pulled out of the airport parking lot.

"In due time. All of your questions will be answered once we board the *Poly-Tech Princess*," Jed McClellan answered as Professor Ali'i turned south on the Kuihelani Highway to head toward the harbor village of Maalaea. "We need some room to spread-out in order for me share with you all a series of astonishing photographs that will blow your cotton-pickin' minds!"

"As for me, Agent McClellan, I'm an *anthropologist*," Dr. Ali'i complained. "My fund of knowledge is devoid of any practical experience concerning historical artifacts."

"In due time," Agent McClellan answered yet again. "Rest assured, your assignment to this team is concerning a parallel course of investigation that you'll undertake that'll likely turn out to be a lot more interesting, and likely a lot more dangerous, than anything that might fall into the realm of experience of either Madam Portal or Professor Harris."

Grover Ali'i glanced in the rear view mirror to briefly scrutinize his now rather alarmed female colleagues residing uncomfortably in the back seat of a somewhat stuffy sedan.

Upon the arrival of the expedition team to the Maalaea Harbor, Professor Ali'i parked his car in a rocky dirt lot on the east side of the port before the four-person task force walked across the main dock where *The Poly-Tech Princess* was moored. As the vessel was gently bobbing up and down in a rhythmical and cyclic fashion, the skipper, Norman Nishioka, was found sitting in a flimsy aluminum lawn chair sipping a tropical cocktail through an impossibly skinny red straw.

Wearing a frayed straw hat and an equally frayed and faded Hilo Hattie Hawaiian blouse, Norman's foot-wear consisted of only a single flip-flop. One could only surmise that the other rubber sandal (that would have otherwise completed the pair) either had suffered an ignominious premature demise from a blow-out, or perhaps the flip-flop had simply slipped off the skipper's foot, danced across the dock under its own volition, and then dove head first into the harbor brine in a premeditated act of suicide to escape the malodorous funk perpetually emanating from the unwashed dogs affixed to Skipper Nishioka's lower extremities below the ankles!

"I don't know how much the Research Institute is paying you to captain this vessel," Professor Ali'i stated, "but whatever it is, I venture it's way too much. What did the chairman tell you about drinking on the job?"

"Take a chill pill, Professor," the skipper replied. "If you must know, this libation happens to be a Mai Tai, fortified with 151 proof Bacardi Rum. As for me, I just love the black-bat logo found on the label of each and every bottle of this high-octane distilled spirit. I have no idea what this symbol of the black bat actually means to the vaunted Bacardi establishment, but as for me, it represents a good time to be had by all!"

"Mai Tai, eh?" Mabel Harris contemptuously inquired when she and Tricia Portal had interjected their unwelcome presence amidst the two men engaged in an up-until-then private conversation, sans invitation, to render an editorial assessment upon the potentially confrontational scenario. "The explorers of old had often scrolled upon their primitive maps a dire warning to all those who had ventured to sail the Seven Seas in search of fame or fortune. 'CAUTION: YONDER MAY DWELL DRAGONS!' Did you know that, Skipper?"

"Do tell," the skipper slurred. "Well, I've got a fire breathing dragon of my own that I'd like to share with you lovely ladies. What's your point?"

"Excellent!" Mabel muttered with a sneer before she turned her head with a sly grin to address her colleague, Tricia Portal. "As I'm foremost an educator, I've stumbled upon a teaching opportunity, Ms. Portal. Time to cast pearls of wisdom to this unkempt heathen. Kick back, relax, and behold a master at the finely-honed craft of humiliating somebody cursed with the possession of a 'Y' chromosome, young lady!"

Mabel narrowed her gaze and refocused her ire upon the skipper. "Now, as for me, I don't want to encounter any pre-historic entities on this excursion, but neither do I want to encounter a barrier reef that would wreck this vessel and leave us stranded somewhere west of Butt-Fuck Timbuktu. Am I making myself clear? If that were to happen, it would likely be a consequence to your currently impaired sensorium, Skipper. Do you honestly think that the excessive consumption of an alcohol-infused adult beverage is actually a good idea right about now, especially if you're indeed planning to navigate this boat to parts unknown?"

"Look lady, I do indeed believe that the consumption of an alcohol-infused adult beverage would be a capital idea right about now. Specifically, a Mai Tai. A *Mai Tai* for *my thigh*! Get it?"

Norm lunged forward in his chair to reach out and grab Tricia Portal by her right wrist. He forcefully pulled her closer to the edge of his lawn chair before leering at her with an overtly lascivious gaze. "My *middle* thigh, to be precise! Get it? Are you game, little sister?"

Alarmed, special agent Jeb McClellan placed his right hand upon his holstered side-arm, just in case the skipper of the *Poly-Tech Princess*, who was now acting like a complete jack-ass, was acutely in need of a severe beat-down. Not to worry, though. After all, it appeared that Ms. Portal was well-versed in the art of hoisting up a tipsy masher by the short hairs just prior to the righteous dispensa-

tion of a much-deserved thrashing if and when such a hostile inter-
lude had ever threatened her well-being.

Tricia leaned forward, and while smiling ever so sweetly, softly whispered into the ear of Skipper Nishioka. "Now, you listen to me you nasty, old, inebriated, fecal-encrusted sod. I don't relish the thought of being out on the ocean in a small boat such as this, and even less so with a dirt bag the likes of you at the helm. If you so much as ever touch me again, I'll hack off your external plumbing with a saw-fish bill and then feed you gonads to a mahi-mahi fish. I'll mummify your putrid, pathetic, and puny pecker and then wear it like a precious pendant around my neck to ward off anybody else who attempts to fuck with me in the future. Have I made myself clear?"

Norm Nishioka reluctantly released Tricia from his grasp and looked down at the perpendicular dock planks without offering a response.

"Well, Norm," Professor Ali'i interjected with a sly grin, "would you like me to introduce you to your other passengers right about now?"

The skipper simply stood up, collapsed his lawn chair before tossing it upon the deck of the catamaran, and then barked out a direct order. "Everybody on board. We're shipping out now. If you want to go the mouth of the Waikono dry river bed, then so be it. I'll pull the stern lines. Grover, you know the drill. Free the bow lines from the dock cleats as soon as I fire up the twin diesels. Dog-walk the beast out of her slip and then jump on at the bow before I throw the tranny into gear. Don't fall into the drink people, because I'm not stopping for shit once we're underway."

As the harbor at Maalaea was more than thirty nautical miles away from the mouth of the Waikono dry river bed in the Kaupo district, *The Poly-Tech Princess* would not likely make it to its destination before night fall. Once the catamaran motored past Ahihi-Kinau natural reserve on the southernmost tip of Maui, it was time for the expedition to get down to business.

"Let's gather around the chart table near the marine head," Jed McClellan instructed. "It's time to put all of the cards on the table so we can bring everybody up to speed on the twin-objectives of this expedition."

Once everybody was present around the small table, the agent opened up a small brief case and pulled out the 1st series of photographs that he wanted to show everybody.

"Excuse me if this proves to be redundant for Professor Mabel Harris and Ms. Tricia Portal, as they've already seen these photographs while we were on a jet plane surfing high above the Pacific in the stratosphere at thirty-five thousand feet. Nonetheless, you certainly haven't seen any of this evidence as of yet, Dr. Ali'i."

Agent McClellan handed out a half dozen 6" x 10" glossy black and white photographs to pass around the table. "These pictures were captured by DOD surveillance hardware in outer space," he continued. "What you're looking at is a bird's-eye view of the mouth of the Waikono dry river bed. When Hurricane Iniki blew by the southern aspect of Maui a month ago, erosion from the storm surge caused a peculiar structure to appear that had been previously buried underneath the river rocks. Tell me what you think this looks like, Professor Ali'i"

"It's a partially exposed, giant, rusty and corroded cigar-shaped object with an obvious propeller shaft extruding from its ass-end," Grover Ali'i correctly observed. "Well, how in hell would I know what it truly might be? A giant, unexploded Japanese torpedo left over from the war in the Pacific?"

"Damnation!" Exclaimed Tricia Portal. "You're a pretty smart guy after all, Professor Ali'i. Well, Dr. Harris, as this is your particular field of expertise, it's now your time for you to shine like a new copper penny. Why don't you spell it out for all of us here at the table as to what we're likely looking at?"

"From the research that I've done thus far, this vessel appears to be consistent with a WWII, Type-A, Ko-hyoteki, two-man Japanese midget assault submarine. These types of submarines were generally armed with two torpedoes," Harris explained. "This is likely a true historical relic."

"That's astonishing!" Ali'i noted.

"As best I can postulate, this sub was sadly lost during the war and ended up on the floor of the dry river bed. What I can't explain however, is how the submarine got buried underneath the river rock, as it would have been quite a task to accomplish such a feat. After all, this type of submarine, when constructed during the war, was over seventy feet long. None of these midget submarines were ever officially named by I.J.N., but they simply had a numerical designation painted upon the vessel's stumpy conning tower, which by these photos, appears to have collapsed directly into the hold of the hull from salt corrosion. Two Japanese naval personnel may have died aboard that sub. If so, the earthly remains of those poor bastards have likely been entombed aboard that doomed vessel for the last 50 years or so," Harris explained.

"Thank you for that rather chilling historical overview as to what we are likely dealing with here, Professor Harris," Dr. Ali'i gratefully stated. The anthropologist turned toward Tricia Portal to ask a pertinent follow-up question. "This doesn't explain what your specific role might be with this situation, Ms. Portal. What stake does the State Department have to do with all of this?"

"Politics."

"Come again?" Ali'i asked for clarification.

"This may turn out to be the big 'October Surprise' in the up-coming presidential election that the Republican Party has been clamoring for! If this pans out as I think it will, it's going to ensure the re-election of President George H.W. Bush. Now that the nasty, jug-eared interloper named H. Ross Perot has thrown his hat into the ring as an independent, he'll likely steal votes away from Bush on election-day. I can't believe it, but my beloved current commander-in-chief might end up passing the presidential baton over to a–a *Democrat*! I shudder at the thought. It's hard for me to fathom that a horny, dope-smoking, unprincipled ridge-runner from some shit-hole, incestuous, one-horse town called Hope, Arkansas, could actually walk away from this next election cycle with the proverbial brass ring. If Bill Clinton ever gets elected, this country will get screwed, both figuratively and literally.

"I don't follow your line of reasoning," Ali'i confessed.

"Although we hammered Saddam Hussein in the Gulf War, the conflict ended a year and a half ago. The public has a short memory. There's now an audible, sub-surface rumbling amongst the great unwashed multitude in America that President Bush might somehow be, well–a *war-monger*, of all things!" Tricia explained.

"You mean he's not?"

"Listen," Tricia continued. "Image is everything. A torpedo bomber that was flown by Bush in WWII was shot down by the Japanese on September 2, 1944. Bush was miraculously saved from the ocean by a nearby American submarine. One would think that Bush would forever hate the Japanese for what happened in WWII."

"Be that as it may, how would our discovery of a fifty-year-old, corroded Japanese war relic have any bearing upon the up-coming presidential election next month?"

"If what we're dealing with here does indeed turn out to be a midget Japanese submarine on the Waikono dry river bed, I'd want to orchestrate a nationally televised re-patriation ceremony to pass over the earthly remains of the I.J.N. personnel, and also the submarine itself, to the Japanese Prime Minister, Miyazawa Kiichi, for all to witness! It would all be non-partisan and above-board, of course," Portal exclaimed.

"Of course," Dr. Ali'i snickered, "but to what end?"

"It would snow—uh, I mean rather, *show* the average, perpetually uninformed American voters that George H.W. Bush has a big heart and that he's truly an all-around, regular, forgive-and-forget, next-door neighbor, nice and decent type of a human being. Do you know what I'm saying? We're talkin' Mom, apple pie, and the American way, by God! A real man of the people, I tell you!" Tricia Portal chirped with unbridled partisan political fervor.

"I've got a head ache!" Grover Ali'i exclaimed. "If for one minute I had ever thought that I was going to be recruited to become a non-paid staff member on the President Bush re-election campaign, I would have stayed home!"

Turning his attention to the naval historian that was sitting across from him, Dr. Ali'i decided to learn a bit more detail about the life of the scholar. "Tell me something, Dr. Harris. How did you possibly become interested in WWII era Naval warfare?"

"Are you asking me that question because I'm black or because I'm a woman?"

"Both, I guess," Ali'i answered with a blush.

"I've come from a long line of Naval warriors, I suppose. During the Civil War, my great-grandfather served in a boiler room, shoveling coal into the furnace of the C.S.S. Richmond. It was one of the original iron clads that was a member-vessel of what was known at the time as the 'Capital Fleet' that helped protect the Confederate seat of governance until the end of the war. After the fall of Petersburg, it was clear that the Federal troops would subsequently storm the Confederate capital. In order to keep the C.S.S. Richmond from falling into the hands of the Yankees, the ship was blown up! My great-grandfather helped pack the kegs of black powder into the hold of the iron clad to facilitate its ultimate destruction. In fact, family tradition denotes that he was likely the very man who lit the damned fuse!"

"What's wrong with this picture?" Ali'i asked. "Are you black?"

"Well," Mabel Harris answered, "I believe so. At least I think I was a black woman the last time I checked."

"Well then," Ali'i pressed," was your great-grandfather black?"

"To the best of my knowledge," Dr. Harris replied with a shrug.

"Then why on earth would he ever want to voluntarily serve in the Confederate Navy aboard a rebel iron clad war ship?" Ali'i asked for clarity.

"I never said that his servitude for the Confederacy was, how should I say, 'voluntary' in any way shape or form. Do I have to spell it out to you?"

"Damn!" Ali'i said, quite shocked. "If that's indeed the case, why is your current main scholarly focus upon WWII if your great-grand-father was involved in the War Between the States?"

"I was only two years old when the Japanese bombed Pearl Harbor. My father was already in the Navy at the time, and he shipped out on a Northampton-class heavy cruiser known as the *USS Houston* at the start of the conflict. His ship was nick-named, the 'Galloping Ghost'. He was in the thick of it right off the bat," Professor Harris answered.

"I didn't think the U.S. military was racially integrated until after WWII, during the Korean War era," McClellan opined. "It was President Truman who established the now sacrosanct military desegregation policy."

"Desperate measures undertaken for desperate times, I suppose," Dr. Harris answered.

"What did your dad do after the war?" Ali'i asked.

"You don't understand," Professor Harris answered as tears began to well in her eyes after a brief pause. "The *USS Houston* and its Australian battle mate, the warship known as the *HMAS Perth,* never returned to their respective home ports."

"What?" Dr. Ali'i asked. "Why not?"

"How should I convey this to you?" Mabel Harris wistfully considered. "As a WWII naval historian, I guess one might say that they're, well—*THEY'RE STILL OUT ON PATROL!*"

"I don't get it," Ali'i said. "The war ended nearly half a century ago. How could these two ships still be 'out on patrol' after all this time?"

It was time for Jed McClellan to defuse the obvious painful remorse and angst that was already gaining a considerable head of steam within the heart and soul of Mabel Harris. "The *Houston* and the *Perth*, along with most of their respective crew members, are now figuratively on patrol in perpetuity at the bottom of the fucking Indian Ocean, you dumb-ass!"

"What?!" Tricia asked.

"Both ships were sunk by the Japanese Imperial Navy on March 1, 1942, during the Battle of the Sunda Strait," McClellan answered. "For shit's sake, ladies and gents! You people really need to learn something about this country that you live in that's called the United States of America."

"I–I'm sorry," Dr. Ali'i muttered as he gazed at the floor. At least he now knew the specific reason as to why Dr. Harris had such a strong affinity for naval warfare history during the historical time frame of WWII. For Dr. Harris, it was, well– *personal.*

"Well," Special Agent McClellan interjected to segue into another topic, "It's time for you all to know the rest of what this mission is all about. There's been a great deal of speculation amongst all of you as to why an armed FBI agent and an anthropologist have been wrangled to go on this mission.

"We're all ears," Tricia Portal said. "What's this secret second agenda that you've been dancing about with an ever-widening, elliptical perimeter?"

"Yes, indeed!" Ali'i exclaimed. "Earlier today, you intimated a gnostic affiliation with a dossier in a less-than-veiled reference to something that apparently has imbued you with an epiphany which we humble mortals are not currently otherwise privy to. Please feel free to enlighten us, G-man. We are, after all, a captive audience, are we not?"

"Let me dial the clock back to when Hurricane Iniki skirted along the southern coast of Maui and the subsequent storm surge washed out the old dirt path known as the St. Isaac's Church Road that provided access to the Akina family ranch well over a month ago. As I previously belabored this matter ad nauseum, the ranch land is now owned by the Feds. When the road cratered, a bull dozer and grader were sent to the site to refurbish the road. It should have been an easy repair, but the project was immediately abandoned."

"Yeah!" Grover Ali'i exclaimed. "After only one day, in fact. What's up with that?"

"Something bad happened," Jeb McClellan explained. "Something *really* bad. What I'm about to tell you is strictly classified information. First, I'll pass around a non-disclosure clause. You three must sign this agreement before we can go any further with what I'm about to reveal to you."

Once Jeb McClellan collected all the non-disclosure forms that had been dutifully signed, he was prepared to proceed with a shocking tale right out of the X-File annals of cryptid hominins. "I have one photograph that was taken by the heavy equipment operator who drove the grader. He captured a solitary picture of his colleague who was operating the big cat dozer at the very moment that this co-worker in question is being clubbed to death by a band of roving primitives. Brace yourselves. What you're about to cast your eyes upon is frankly, rather disturbing!"

McClellan passed around the black-and-white photograph for everybody to evaluate before pulling a set of printed notes from his brief to accurately relay the events regarding this particular forthcoming tale of horror.

"The operator of the grader stated that his co-worker on the big cat dozer was only about twenty yards ahead of him on the dirt road when it happened. In his own words, and I quote, 'About a dozen or so butt-naked, angry little midgets jumped out from the adjacent kiawe grove, climbed upon the dozer, pulled off Charlie's hard hat, and then clubbed the poor sumbitch in the head until they crushed his fucking skull! One of the little bastards, and then another, bit Charlie in the face, tearing off the right side of his face below his eye socket. These nasty little monsters then gobbled down several chunks of Charlie's flesh.' Wow! Can you people in this chart room fathom that scenario?"

"He was, what—dragged off and then eaten alive?!" Tricia Portal asked with considerable alarm.

"Presumably so." McClellan continued. "Wait! I'm not done. Let me finish the written testimony that I've been reading to you thus far. Again, I quote, 'The project manager had given me a camera that morning, as it's customary to capture a before and after picture to confirm that the commissioned work had been property completed by the end of the day. That's how I captured the snap of Charlie getting his brains bashed in. Go ahead. Develop the film. I'll never look at it. I lived through it, and I don't need to see an instant replay of Charlie getting murdered. After they hauled off Charlie's body into the thicket, they started to give me the stink-eye. As best I could tell, I was going to be next on the menu! I didn't even bother to turn off the ignition switch for the diesel engine that powered the grader before I jumped down from the wheel and ran away as if my balls were on fire! My pickup was parked at the unmarked intersection of Piilani and that old dirt church road. The angry little midgets were in hot pursuit the whole way, but I dived into the unlocked cab with only seconds to spare. As I fired up my F-150 and threw it into gear to beat a hasty retreat, my truck was pelted with projectiles that the little spear-chuckers hurled in my direction. I ain't ever going back, I tell you!' Well, ladies and gents, that's the end of the narrative. What do you say to that?"

"There must be more to the story," Dr. Harris protested. "What else is in your secret dossier?"

"The National Guard was called out to the Saint Isaac's Church Road the following day to only discover that the heavy equipment had been torched," McClellan answered. "The road grade operator who escaped the assault without injury wants to remain anonymous, but he nonetheless reported that the stature of the band of assailants was on average of only about four and a half feet tall, although very muscular. The photo experts at Quantico confirmed that none of these naked little people were above five feet in height."

"So," Grover Ali'i asked, "all the evidence thus far is only photographic except for an alleged solitary eye-witness testimony?"

"It was a *sworn* testimony, I'll have you know. What else do you want?" McClellan answered with a tinge of irritation. "If you ever saw a victim dying in agony with a spear thrust into his breadbasket, would that be enough evidence for you, Professor?"

"Now, that's a bit harsh," Grover Ali'i protested.

"Oh, really? This situation is exactly why you're here, Dr. Ali'i. Uncle Sam has issued a command performance request from an anthropologist, and you fit the bill. Take a look at the photo and offer a reasonable hypothesis, based upon your background in the rather obscure discipline of human ethnic and sub-racial morphology, as to who these people are and where they might have originally come from," Jeb McClellan stated before passing a magnifying glass to the professor.

After Grover Ali'i scrutinized the photograph, he leaned back in his chair and expanded his cheeks before he expelled the air out his lungs with an equine-like sputter from his lips. "These people appear to have the stature, cutaneous pigmentation, broad facial features, and peppercorn hair of the Pygmy Tribe from the sub-Saharan Congo region in Africa. The main difference is that these individuals, at least the ones that we see in the photograph, appear to be quite robust. Of course who ever these people are, they can't really be from the continent of Africa, as there's no real hard evidence to date that the indigenous people from Africa were sea-faring, much less possessing the where-with-all to cross the entire Indian Ocean and then far into Northern Pacific, literally half-way around the world."

"I find that to be a rather prejudicial opinion coming from you, Professor Ali'i," Dr. Harris protested. "Of course, they're Pygmies! As a black woman, I say that with great pride, as a matter of fact. As far as people from the continent of Africa lacking the technical ability to set sail across the Ocean in prehistoric times, that's an absolute fallacy. Did you already forget the personal story that I told you about the fact that I've come from a long line of naval warriors?"

"A one-off the assembly line happenstance in your own particular situation certainly doesn't capture a societal phenomenon of a specific sub-race of humans from another part of the world," Ali'i countered.

"Do you personally dispute the fact that the Melanesian people are of African origin?" Dr. Harris asked. "Besides, how far is the Congo region of Africa from the coast of the Indian Ocean? Five hundred miles? A thousand miles? Do you have the audacity to sit there and tell me that the people of equatorial Africa didn't have the where-with-all to hike that far to the sea shore and subsequently launch exploratory expeditions into the ocean blue?"

"Who are the Melanesian people?" Tricia Portal asked.

"As their ethnic name sake would imply," Ali'i answered, "this heavily pigmented group of individuals predominantly occupy Fiji, New Guinea, Papua, the Solomon Islands, and Vanuatu. Now, is Dr. Harris correct in her supposition that these people are of African origin? I dispute that likelihood, but as for now, who really knows."

"How could that ever be determined?" Jeb McClellan asked.

"Two years ago this very month, the international scientific research community launched the Human Genome Project on October 1, 1990. The NIH predicts it will take about fifteen more years of research before the genetic code of Homo sapiens will be completely analyzed. Once done, we'll be able to sort out specific migration patterns of our remote ancestors. However, I think we'll likely be deep into the next millennia until we're able to answer the question as to whether the Melanesian people are actually of African origin or not."

"Bullshit!" Dr. Harris retorted. "We don't need future data from the Human Genome Project to know what's going on here.

Phenotype is a direct reflection of genotype. Period. These people in this photograph are Pygmies, I tell you!"

"I dispute that proclamation!" Ali'i vehemently protested. "The phenomenon of parallel evolution refutes your hypothesis. Now look, I have myopia. I wear reading glasses. If I take off my glasses, at a distance of only 50 paces, I wouldn't be able to discern a ten foot dolphin from a ten foot tiger shark!"

"What's your point?" Dr. Harris asked.

"Can't you see?" Ali'i responded. "Now, one of these creatures is an intelligent mammal, and the other is a primitive cartilaginous fish with a puny brain that's about the size of a walnut. Nonetheless, both of these aquatic animals share a similar, gross, generalized, external appearance, do they not? Any guess as to the reason being? It's only because they share the same *environment,* boys and girls. That's why."

"Well, maybe, but–"

"No 'but' about it," Dr. Ali'i said to rudely cut off his colleague. "Another matter is that the Pygmy Tribe has never been accused of *cannibalism*. Now, I can't say the same about some of the other tribes that have been engaged in open warfare against the Pygmy people from time to time, but Pygmies have never been observed to actually eat their fellow human beings. As a basic anthropological tenet to which I adhere, that's a societal trait that in all likelihood, is gen-erationally passed on as an in-grained, moral tradition amongst a cohesive tribal group of people, and one that is remarkably and pre-dictably consistent over time!"

"Thank you for that scholarly dissertation, Professor, but you didn't answer the question," the FBI agent asked as a point of con-tention. "What's going on here? If the truth be told, I think you *know* what we're dealing with. You're just afraid to voice what's the only realistic remaining possibility, no matter how improbable it might sound to your own ear, or to anybody else for that matter. What's the problem, Ali'i? Think that your sterling academic reputation might somehow get tarnished if you say it out loud?"

"If the solitary photograph that you have shown us is the only image I can readily scrutinize, then I'm certainly unable to pigeonhole this particular tribe. They have the stature of Pygmies, the broad facial features of the more widely-dispersed Bantu people, but thinner lips, much more like the Cushite people. Perhaps they're actually of Indo-European origin, not African," Ali'i postulated.

"Wait!" Dr. Harris said. "What of their dark cutaneous pigmentation? What about the texture and color of their hair?"

"That's no help." Ali'i said. "Melanin content only suggests an affiliation with a tropical climate and nothing else as far as I'm concerned. Hair color and texture are certainly not uniform features even amongst people of the same ethnic or racial group. As a case in point, Dr. Dr. Harris, you have somewhat reddish-tinged hair, but you are nonetheless African-American. The one thing that really confounds me about this group is an apparent, profoundly muscular, body habitus. Either this tribe is juiced-up on anabolic steroids and pumps iron at the local gym on a daily basis, or we're looking at a true biological variance. In any event, I have absolutely no other ethnic or racial comparative point of reference."

"A completely new ethnic group, maybe?" Jeb McClellan asked. "Well, they must have migrated from *somewhere*."

"If we have indeed encountered a previously unrecognized paleolithic tribe, I would surmise that these people may be a derivative of the legendary diminutive warrior tribe from Sumatra known to the locals there as the Orang Pendek," Ali'i professed to his team members but without any true intellectual conviction.

"Even *you* can't believe that, Dr. Ali'i!" McClellan exclaimed. "If the Orang Pendek truly exist, they'd most likely fit the bill as a previously unrecognized, diminutive *hominid* primate, not a *hominin*! If the Orang Pendek are indeed dwelling in the jungles of Sumatra, and I believe they are, they're definitely *not* some human relic."

"You know this how, Agent McClellan?" Tricia Portal asked.

"Uncle Sam knows a lot of things we'll never share with the American people," Jeb answered before turning back to Professor Ali'i. "Anytime you're ready to tell us your *real* opinion, and not some line of horse manure, your colleagues and I are indeed eager to hear what you honestly have to say!"

While his two female colleagues scrutinized the professor with great interest, no answer from Grover Ali'i was readily forthcoming despite a prolonged silent pause. Nonetheless, pertinent questions also remained about the agenda of the FBI agent in their midst.

"The skipper has just down-throttled the twin diesels," Professor Ali'i ascertained. "We must be getting close to the mouth of the Waikono dry river bed. Why did the Feds fly you out here, Agent McClellan? The FBI has a primary office in Honolulu and there's also an adjunct over on Main in Wailuku. Are not the local agents within the confines of the local Hawaiian community smart enough to handle a job like this?"

"Frankly, no," the gumshoe replied. "They most certainly are *not* up to the task."

"So," Dr. Harris pressed, "what exactly made you, how should I say, a first round draft choice in the position of a center line-backer for the illustrious bureau?"

"I'm the go-to guy for any regional aboriginal conflicts that may arise from time to time, McClellan boasted."

"Say what?" Tricia Portal asked.

"Take for example as to how I specifically handled the Hogama Tribe up-rising in Abernod County back on July 4, 1988. Thirteen at-large tribal members barged into an Elk Lodge celebration to protest what they perceived to be 'taxation without representation'.

They were also perturbed by their perception of the *alleged* fracture of a specific bilateral treaty, as a consequence to duplicitous actions undertaken by the United States government."

"Just to think moments ago you specifically accused me of ignorance concerning important details regarding American history," professor Ali'i muttered under his breath.

"What?" McClellan asked. "I'm sorry, but did you just say something, Professor?"

"No," Ali'i said as he cleared his throat. "Please continue with your captivating story. Thus far, your tale has been a real killer story, if you catch my meaning."

"I was able to coax the belligerent hostiles to come out from the lodge meeting in a peaceful manner. They were immediately greeted by heavily armed members of the ATF who promptly gunned down every one of those radical freaks to the very last man. Can't have anybody refusing to pay taxes in this country. That won't happen. After all, the tax code is to the secular, humanistic, godless, and morally bankrupt Democratic Party as to what the sacrament of the Eucharist is to confirmed papists."

"You're preaching to the choir over here," Tricia Portal said with a methodical nod.

"Taxation is a weapon. After all, it's the primary punitive tool that the government utilizes to suppress the freedoms of the people that live in this country. Everybody has to pay their 'fair share'," McLellan confirmed.

"I've heard that line of crap from liberals all my life," Mabel Harris said. "What exactly is the 'fair share' that I, as an American, must be forced to pay?"

"Whatever the fuck Uncle Sam says that it is," McClellan laughed. "It's an arbitrary high percentage of whatever meager possession a person such as yourself may actually try to own in this miserable life!"

"It's sad that our inalienable freedoms and rights are currently infringed upon by the Feds, don't you think so?" Dr. Harris queried aghast.

"Smell the coffee, Dr. Harris! Freedom is nothing but a myth. An opiate for the masses, I tell you. It hasn't existed in this country for a long time," McClellan casually replied. "Get over it! As a case in point, there's a hostile religious organization that was formed by a man named Benjamin Roden back in 1955. They call themselves the 'Branch Davidians'. They have a large communal compound near Waco called the New Mount Carmel Center."

"Who are these people now, and why would the government consider them to be a threat?" Dr. Ali'i asked.

"Separatists, I tell you!" the agent exclaimed. "I swear to God, if those crazy-ass people look at the Federal government sideways just one more time, we'll send a team down to Texas with our guns a-blazin', kill everybody there, and then burn the whole goddamned place right down to the ground!"

"What about the image of the naked, primitive warriors captured on the photograph taken near the Waikono river bed?" Tricia asked. "What is your specific intent concerning this presumed isolated tribe?"

"Frankly, I'm surprised that you don't know the details about this specific aspect of the mission, Ms. Portal," agent Jeb McClellan stated. "After all, this particular edict came directly from members of the deep state hiding in plain site within the confines of your very own department. I have been specifically instructed to make peaceful contact with these primitive savages and ascertain the location of their village if they do indeed have one. I'll then relay the geographical coordinates to the commando specialists at the Schofield Barracks. In short order, a team will be shipped out here to the Kaupo district to take care of the problem once and for all."

"You can't do that!" Professor Ali'i exclaimed. "If this particular band of warriors that assaulted the bulldozer and road grader operators are indeed from a primitive, paleolithic tribe as the case may be, they no doubt reacted out of pure fear towards monstrous, earth-moving internal combustion machinery that they had likely never seen before! In addition, human beings are tribal and fearful by nature, and collectively, we tend to mistrust other people that may be cut from a different ethnic or racial bolt of cloth!"

"I disagree with that hypothesis, Professor Ali'i," Dr. Harris countered. "Just take a look at the constitution of this intrepid band of explorers that are all working in relative harmony toward one common objective. Within this very group, we have one black, two Caucasians, one Pacific Islander, and an Oriental skipper."

"The preferred term is now 'Asian', not 'Oriental'," Skipper Nishioka espoused as he hopped down the gang way from his post at the helm. "You're wrong Dr. Harris. If the truth be told, I for one can't stand to be around any one of you sanctimonious sons-of-bitches!"

"Thanks for the lovely house-boat party that you've hosted for our benefit," Tricia said sarcastically. "I can't speak on behalf of my colleagues, however I've had quite a delightful time up until now! Should I start looking for that razor-sharp nose bill from a sawfish that I spoke of earlier, Captain?"

Skipper Nishioka neglected to offer a response to Ms. Portal's inflammatory comment. "Now, the ocean is quite calm and we'll be at the mouth of the Waikono in just a few. I'll pull up on the rocky shore line just long enough for you people to jump out from the bow. Once you're in the clear, I'll throw the *Princess* into reverse, back off about one hundred fifty feet which is just beyond the breakers, and then I'll drop anchor there. Whatever you're now doing down here in the hold, wrap it up and grab your gear. All ashore in five!"

"You heard the man!" Jeb McClellan barked. "Saddle up, people. It's time to bail."

"Wait one damned minute!" Professor Ali'i protested. "We're not done here yet! Not by a long shot. Moments ago, you previously mentioned that there's a military assault team waiting in the weeds to exterminate these people if we find them. That would be murder! That would be a sin! That would be the genocide of an entire ethnic group of people that we know absolutely nothing about. They've probably been living here in the shadows of modernity for eons as a self-sufficient, paleolithic tribe!"

"You're absolutely right, Professor!" Agent McClellan scoffed. "If they're living out here off the grid without any comprehension of a capitalistic economic model, or conversely, they're currently unencumbered by a 'helping hand' offered by an intrusive, progressive, and paternalistic government welfare system, then that's exactly why they'd need to completely disappear! Can't have that! No sir-eee, Grover! You see, if that were indeed the case, we wouldn't be able to tax them! If we can't tax them, then we certainly can't control them. What would you expect Uncle Sam to do then? Just simply let these primitives live out here as free as the proverbial bird of paradise, independent from all the glorious benefits of the modern American Dream?"

"I can't believe what I'm hearing with my own ears!" Dr. Mabel Harris said.

"A primitive stone age tribe is indeed out there," Jeb McClellan said. "You people need to think of these evil little savages as an 'invasive species'. Nothing more, and nothing less. This tribe is just like the nasty-ass, big-thorn kiawe tree that grows like a weed on the leeward side of this island. The kiawe is a documented invasive species, erroneously introduced to this island chain long ago. The filthy kiawe tree, if ever encountered, needs to be uprooted and then the residual stump needs to be burned out, just before the dirt from which it grew is sterilized with gallons of carcinogenic herbicidal poisons, and then covered in salt! We're talkin' a formal, government mandated, barren, moon-scape policy over here, people! This primitive tribe, if and when encountered, should be treated in a similar aggressive fashion, I tell ya'!"

"You're the one on this expedition who's indeed an evil savage!" Ali'i fumed.

"Spare my life! This couldn't possibly a feeble attempt at an insult emanating from the mouth of a man who self-identifies as being of *Polynesian* descent, now could it?!" The G-man sneered at Grover Ali'i before turning to Mabel Harris. "As for your own personal, goody-two-shoes incredulity, Dr. Harris, *I'm* the one who can't believe what I'm hearing with *my* own ears!"

"So, what's your game, Agent McClellan?" Ali'i asked with furrowed brow. "Looks as if you're trying to pick a fight for no particular reason, are you not? Sounds like you've got a bone to pick with me, and a big one to boot. If that's the case, just lay it on the line, won't you?"

"You're a fool, Grover Ali'i, and a hypocritical one at that!"

"What?!" Ali'i responded to the affront. "Did you just call me a hypocrite?"

"You heard me," the FBI agent stated. "Time to get down to the brass tacks, amigo! Out of respect for the very fact that you are indeed of Polynesian descent, I'll give you this one last chance to tell your fellow colleagues about what we're dealing with out here before I spill the beans. If you make me say it, you and your ancestors will certainly be painted in a most unfavorable and embarrassing light of reprehensible scorn."

"Stop!" Ali'i protested. "Are you expecting me to recite an act of contrition in front of a church altar for-for some remote crimes that I never even personally committed?"

"Do it! You damn well know the name of this primitive tribe that attacked those heavy equipment operators. Just say it, you coward! Before a man can find redemption, or perhaps even salvation after this life, I believe that the collective sins of one's ancient ancestors must not only be acknowledged, but they must also be publicly confessed to the congregation of the faithful who may be present in order for them to simply bear witness!"

"THE MENEHUNE!" Professor Ali'i screamed out before he turned his head and looked away in shame. "The Menehune," he now repeated as little more than a soft whimper. "There. I said it. Hope you're happy, G-man. Are we done now?"

WIFE BEATER

CHAPTER 2

WHAT'S ON THE MENU?

After the expeditionary team gathered upon the foredeck, Jeb McClellan meandered back toward the helm to chat with Norman Nishioka. "Have you found a place yet to reach the bow-end and allow us to disembark, Skipper?"

"Can't you see I'm working on it? The *Princess* is a cat that's powered by twin in-line diesel in-board four cylinder engines with two fixed-shaft out-drives. I've got to find a steep embankment coming off of the rocky shore, or else I'll butcher the props. If that happens, it'll be a long walk back to Maalaea."

"If any trouble should happen, I guess you could always just call the Coast Guard," the FBI agent said hopefully.

"Sorry. Not on this voyage, G-man!" Norman exclaimed.

"What?" Jeb asked. "The local field office is going to expect a call from me if I stumble upon something important out here."

"Something important like, oh, I don't know—the Menehune, maybe? Believe you me, Agent McClellan. They're indeed out there. My grandfather saw them harvest a feral pig out in the forest above the Kula district, back in the thirties! Don't worry, though. You don't have to look for *them.* If you wander off into their territory, they'll

41

find *you*. I hope if any encounter does indeed occur, they remain tranquil and passive. If they fly off the handle, as they've been known to do from time to time, they can become extraordinarily violent. We won't be able to call for backup if that happens, as the two-way is on the fritz."

"You know about the Menehune?" Agent McClellan asked. "Why didn't you say something, damn it?"

"You never asked," the skipper replied. "I've heard the stories as most folks have, who know anything about the history of these islands."

"You must also be referring to the historically recorded event, now known as the George London affair, that happened in the Waimea Valley back in the 1940s after the war." Agent McClellan said.

"Yes," Skipper Nishioka confirmed, "but there's a lot more encounters that occurred in the past above and beyond what a bunch of kids from George London's classroom had witnessed during an elementary school field trip to the forests in northern Oahu all those years ago."

"Care to elaborate?" Jeb asked.

"Check this out, gum-shoe," the skipper added. "Local rumors also suggest that the Menehune still inhabit the windward side of the Big Island. There's more. My second cousin even told me that his sister-in-law had personally witnessed a hunting party of the Menehune patrolling the Kalalau Valley in Kauai years ago. Who knows?"

"So, after you drop anchor offshore," Jeb McClellan asked hopefully, "would you want to jump into the drink and swim up to the rocky coast to join our expedition?"

"I'll pass!" Nishioka stated in no uncertain terms. "You see, I'm of Japanese ancestry. When my late older brother was just a teen, he heard the stories about a Japanese submarine that had previously crashed into the shores on this relatively uninhabited side of the island during the war. Allegedly, two submariners were eventually captured by the Menehune tribe. Several rather unpleasant reports abound as to what exactly happened to those two sailors."

"Nothing good, I'd venture," McClellan opined.

"I plan to just hang out here on the deck of the *Princess* and keep a low profile. As you all have sleeping bags, you'll likely want to spend the night on shore before you get an early start for your expedition," the skipper told the agent before handing him a large, metal, basketball-referee whistle. "Keep this whistle. When you want me to pick you up, blow that damned thing, and blow it hard. I'll be able to hear you, and I'll come pick you up before the cannibals hunt you down and eat you for dinner!"

"Thanks!" Agent McClellan exclaimed. "One last light-hearted question before I depart. The exhaust from your two diesel engines has the unmistakable delicious odor of a deep-fried, red and green chili chimichanga from a Taco Hell fast food restaurant. What's up with that?"

"About twenty years ago, the liberal News Tweeker magazine ran a ridiculous article about the worldwide risk of global cooling as a consequence to the carbon dioxide that was being dumped into the atmosphere because of our reliance upon fossil fuels and the infernal internal combustion engines utilized in our modern society," Skipper Nishioka explained. "The Board of Regents at the Research Institute issued a mandate over a decade ago that all of our research vessels were to be propelled by bio-diesel, which we now locally refine at our own labs from the used cooking oil we purchase, at a great expense I might add, from near-by Hawaiian restaurants."

"What a great idea!" McClellan said.

"What a load of crap!" the skipper proffered as a retort. "That bio-diesel horse-piss costs three times the amount of money that we'd otherwise pay for conventional diesel fuel that comes out of the fuel pump from the marina at the Maalaea Harbor!"

The skipper squinted at the coast, as it appeared that he found the specific landing site that he was looking for. "Heads up, Jeb. I've found a sharp slope dropping away from the shore that I can easily glide into. Get your team ready to boogie on out of here."

"What's the matter, Skip?" McClellan asked with a wink and a chuckle as he headed back toward the bow. "Don't you want to save the world from the catastrophic calamity of man-made climate change by using an environmentally safer power source like bio-diesel, as opposed to the toxic fossil fuels that we suck out of our beloved Gaia?"

"Who in hell is Gaia?" the skipper asked.

"Mother Earth," Jeb answered. "In ancient Greek mythology, she's also known as the Mother of Uranus!"

"As for now," Nishioka bellowed, "you can take that whistle and shove it up *your anus*, G-man. Now, get you and your crew the royal fuck off my boat!"

The expedition team disembarked upon the rocky shore a quarter of a mile West of the Waikono dry river bed which traversed immediately parallel to the now-decommissioned dirt road cut off from the Piilani Highway to the structural remnants of the lost Russian colony and church.

"I'm eager to see the ship wreckage!" Dr. Harris exclaimed. "As of yet, the sun hasn't set. It might be sinking a bit low on the horizon, but I'll wager that if we hump it, we can get to the river bed while there's still a bit of daylight left."

When the crew climbed upon a fifteen foot ridge immediately adjacent to the shoreline, it was quite evident that the task at hand would be rougher than anticipated.

"I can tell you right now, Dr. Harris, there's no way in hell that we can safely make it to the river bed at this late hour," Dr. Ali'i warned as he bent down to carefully pick up a rather nasty broken scrub branch that was festooned with an array of three inch, iron-hard, and incredibly sharp barbs. "This is what we'd be up against. We'd be facing a treacherous hike through a big-thorn, kiawe grove. The kiawe is a brutal, non-native, invasive tree. It's actually in the mesquite family, to the best of my limited knowledge concerning tropical flora and fauna. I stepped on a thorn from one of these plants a few years ago, and it pierced the sole of my shoe! The damned toxin-impregnated spike punctured all the way through my foot, exiting the top of my shoe, I tell you! I ended up with cellulitis and systemic sepsis that got me hospitalized for more than a week at the Maui Memorial. If it gets dark and we're out there stumbling about through that grove, we all could get into some serious trouble in a hurry."

"The professor is right," McClellan said. "Let's breakout are bed rolls on top of this ridge and start a fire. We'll get a fresh start in the morning."

Jeb McClellan wasn't hungry in the least, but he had the courtesy to pull out three MRE boxes to share with his team members so they wouldn't go to sleep on an empty stomach. While sitting around the small camp fire and dining on their humble provisions, it was time for Tricia Portal to break the ice and broach the subject concerning the most-unpleasant verbal exchange that had occurred between Dr. Ali'i and the FBI agent just before the team had departed the relative safety of *Poly-Tech Princess.*

"Who were the Menehune, Professor Ali'i," Tricia asked, "and what did your Polynesian ancestors have to do with these people?"

"Many of my less-than-collegial intellectual contemporaries don't even believe that the race of Menehune actually ever existed, but I certainly do," the professor explained. "Through oral tradition, the Menehune were described as the 'Little People' who occupied the Hawaiian chain prior to the arrival of the Polynesian migrants from Tahiti over a thousand years ago or so. For whatever reason, bloody internecine warfare erupted between the two different races of people."

"How could an open, bloody war *not* break out between the Polynesian and Menehune tribe?" Jeb McClellan interjected with an inappropriate chuckle. "Dr. Ali'i and I might not agree on much, but we've both already espoused our humble opinions that human beings are generally distrustful of other people who look, talk, or think differently than members of their own, personal tribal group!"

"Well, Dr. Ali'i," Dr. Harris asked with obvious trepidation, "what, uh–what do you think happened in the end?"

"My Polynesian ancestors likely exterminated the Menehune as a race," Dr. Ali'i sheepishly answered. "At least I thought that was the case, up until Special Agent McClellan passed around a photograph earlier today revealing a heavy-equipment operator sitting upon a bull dozer who was getting viciously clubbed to death by a band of violent, naked midgets!"

"Do you truly think there are still any stone-age people living in the shadows on this crowded planet of ours that's already bursting at the seams?" Dr. Harris asked.

"Hands down," Ali'i replied. "In 1956, the North Sentinel Island in the Indian Ocean was declared a reserve for a paleolithic tribe that lives there to this very day. These people apparently have not had any interaction with the outside world, and it's now forbidden for anybody to ever go there now. A team of anthropologists had previously gone to this particular island, and the scientists who went on that ill-fated exploratory probe had simply disappeared."

"Sad, but true," McClellan said.

"There's more," Ali'i added. "At an anthropology seminar I attended in 1989, I personally met a guest speaker who was a Russian geologist named Ivan Petrov. This man was captured near the Amazon basin in Brazil by a previously unknown tribe of head-hunters, and the good professor was held captive and brutally tortured for nineteen days."

"Must be ancient history," Dr. Harris said.

"No!" Ali'i said. "This was a contemporary event that occurred in modern times! As I recall, this traumatic tale happened back around 1981. That's only eleven years ago, boys and girls!"

"I find this hard to believe," Dr. Harris said.

"I shit you not!" Ali'i answered. "This newly discovered tribe has subsequently been identified as a remote and isolated subset of the Tagaeri people of the rain forest, based purely upon their recorded dialect following additional contact with this isolated population in the mid-80s. After Ivan Petrov was captured, the niece of a tribal elder had become quite ill with a high fever. The professor assumed that the young woman was likely infected with malaria. Fortunately, her physical health had dramatically rallied after Dr. Petrov shared his own personal supply of hydroxychloroquine with the young woman. This heads-up intervention from the geologist likely spared him from ending up in the lower digestive tract of these primitive head-hunters!"

"As an anthropologist," Tricia Porter interjected, "you must be excited about the prospects of meeting a race of people that otherwise had been thought to be extinct up until now!"

"I'm not so damned sure about that," Dr. Ali'i said as he flipped over on his bed roll to turn his face away from the crackling camp fire. "After all, I'm Polynesian. My forefathers came from Tahiti. If I actually encountered a remnant clan of the Menehune race that somehow escaped extermination at the hands of my Polynesian ancestors, this lost tribe would surely be able to readily ascertain as to *who* and *what* I truly am."

"What are you saying?" Tricia asked. "How could they possibly know who your ancestors might have been, Polynesian or otherwise?"

"If they had an opportunity to scrutinize my rather distinct facial features, you'd actually contend that they wouldn't be able to figure all of that out?" Ali'i opined. "If and when that perilous happenstance were to ever occur, these people, whoever they might be, could actually believe that yours truly is somehow guilty of the very sins committed by my ancestors, as previously professed by Special Agent McClellan."

"Much like the Roman Catholic concept of the 'Original Sin' that has infiltrated the psyche of the members of that particular branch of Christianity with eons of perpetual self-doubt and guilt?" Tricia Portal thought aloud.

"Precisely," Grover Ali'i agreed. "If that were indeed the case and my Polynesian lineage is ever revealed to this tribe in a future face-to-face encounter, no matter how brief, there's no doubt that I'd likely have hell to pay, and then some! I just hope that I taste good, if in the end, these blood-thirsty little bastards decide to eat me..."

The four members of the expedition team had awakened at day break from the sound of old C & W music blaring from a cassette player that was affixed to the deck of the *Poly-Tech Princess*, which was dutifully and firmly anchored in the plate-glass smooth ocean waters immediately off shore. It should have been no surprise to anybody present that the specific first song that Skipper Nishioka had queued-up on the cassette player was none other than the unofficial anthem of the chronically inebriated. The song was, "Pop A Top", which was originally a hit record by Jim Ed Brown back in 1966.

"Wake-up people!" the skipper barked toward the shore from a bull horn. "Pack up your shit and hike eastward. You're only about four hundred yards or so from the Waikono dry river bed. Watch your step! When you get back to this spot, blow the referee's whistle and I'll pick you up. Now, get goin'!"

"I hate that guy," Tricia muttered.

"I for one hate Country and Western music," Mabel Harris added. "The skipper needs to turn that crap off. He's playing it loud enough to wake the dead!"

Well, perhaps the skipper wasn't really playing his favorite music loud enough to wake the dead, but perhaps it was just loud enough to awaken the nearby Menehune. Unfortunately, as it would soon turn out, Norman Nishioka would learn a painful lesson that most of the members of this particular paleolithic tribe were not particularly fond of Country and Western genre, either...

On the shoreline, the team packed up their gear, and carefully weaved their way through the kiawe grove toward the mouth of the Waikono dry river bed. On the way, Tricia Portal found the stump of a broken tree branch that could fit within the palm of her hand. The broken branch was adorned with an enormous, four inch long, solitary, stiletto-like, kiawe thorn. She elected to keep it in her back-pack as a souvenir, completely unaware that it would most likely get confiscated at the airport if and when she would ever have an opportunity to fly back to the mainland.

Upon clearing the tree line, the team had entered a flat, broad pasture that comprised an area of about three acres. "We've crossed into what was once the Akina family ranch. This particular area of the ranch was the location of the lost Russian colony that disappeared for some mysterious reason way back in the early 1800s. If you look to your right, you'll see a lava rock foundation upon a short cinder cone that's approximately forty feet by twenty-five feet in its perimeter dimension. This is all that remains of what was once the Russian Orthodox Church that was built on this site nearly two centuries ago. I've searched this location several times, and I still don't know exactly what happened to the Russian colony."

"Bullshit, Professor! By now, you and I both know exactly what happened to the missing Russian settlers. I have no doubt in my mind that it's also the same, exact, ignominious fate that had sadly befallen the Akina family that once owned this ranch. It seems you readily admit that the Menehune still exist as a paleolithic race, but what will it take for you to admit that Menehune are indeed, well—*evil?*" Jeb McClellan pressed for an answer.

"Special Agent McClellan," Professor Ali'i said as he stopped in his tracks. "Being *evil* and being *frightened* are two different things. I for one do believe that the Menehune are out there, and that they're *frightened* of our modern technology, but that does not necessarily make them *evil*, per se. You must truly think the very worst of your fellow human beings, both modern and primitive, now don't you?"

"Grow up, Professor! Do you somehow dispute the fact that the Menehune actively participate in cannibalism? Is that not considered to be *evil* by almost all human racial and ethnic groups upon the face of this planet? It was just last night when you uttered the opinion that the members of the Menehune tribe were 'blood-thirsty little bastards'. Your words, pal—not mine!"

"I don't recall saying that," Ali'i lied.

"Well, you said those very words last night, and you were spot-on, as far as I'm concerned! The Menehune are not only, blood-thirsty little bastards as you stated, but they're also *evil*."

"If cannibalism is an accepted pan-tribal societal norm for these paleolithic people, do we actually have the right to impose our belief systems upon them as to what may be *good* or what may be *evil?*" Ali'i asked.

"Oh, for fuck's sake!" Tricia Portal interjected. "We have a progressive liberal in our midst! You people are so spiritually and intellectually devoid of common sense, you couldn't possibly even recognize the evidentiary proof that something *evil* actually exists, even if it was looking you right in the eye!"

"So it would seem," McClellan added in agreement. The G-man proceeded to repeat a specific verbatim rhetorical question to Grover Ali'i that was asked the previous day. "If ever you saw a victim dying in agony with a spear thrust into his breadbasket, would that be enough evidence for you, Professor?"

Meanwhile, a breeze from the North started to gently rock the *Poly-Tech Princess* while Norman Nishioka enthusiastically sipped upon a Bloody Mary, early-morning, 'eye-opener' cocktail. Norm preferred his Bloody Mary beverages concocted with gin, not vodka. There was just something about the nasty taste and foul odor of fermented juniper berries that reminded him of the nauseating stench from the jet-fuel vapors that he had become so accustomed to inhaling during the waning days of the late Viet Nam War.

The skipper suddenly turned off the cassette player that continued to bellow out obscure Country and Western Music from the remote past, as the sound of repeated splashing water was unexpectedly detected from the port side of the boat.

"Something has come to visit me! Spinner dolphins, I venture. I love the spinner dolphins," the skipper chuckled. "They taste like chicken!"

Norman Nisioka leaned over the port side railing to peer into the deep. From the now frothy blue ocean, a spear tip that had been fashioned from volcanic glass was thrust into the skipper's corpulent anterior neck. Norm made a futile gasp and gurgling protest before he was pulled over the railing by his assailants, who were subsequently able to dispatch with the skipper and dismember him into tasty, bite-size morsels!

It all happened so fast, that no clear forensic trace of the foul deed would ever be found aboard the catamaran, except for the eventual curious discovery of the fractured port-side boat railing near the bow of the vessel.

As the team of explorers proceeded to cross the open pasture, they found the washed-out and heavily rutted St. Isaac's Church Road, adjacent to the Waikono dry river bed.

"Heads up, people," the G-man cautioned. "This is the exact location where the heavy-equipment operators were attacked when they tried to repair the road wash-out caused by Hurricane Iniki. We must presume that there are indeed eyes on the trail. I suggest that we cross this path to the other side as quickly as possible."

Fortunately, the St. Isaac's Church Road was traversed without difficulty or incident. "I no longer hear Skipper Nishioka's infernal hill-billy music," Dr. Harris observed after she ran across the trail.

Everybody laughed when Tricia Portal added, "I bet the neighbors pounded on his door and ordered him to pipe down that God-awful, red-neck noise!"

After only hiking about thirty yards up the dry river bed, the carcass of a badly corroded WWII Japanese miniature assault submarine was readily in sight. With great excitement, Dr. Harris and Tricia Portal ran ahead to scrutinize the important military artifact.

"Looks like I found the 'October Surprise' that's going to get President George H.W. Bush re-elected!" Tricia beamed.

"Looks like I'll be granted tenure at my university once I get an article published in the next month's *Slings and Arrows* specialty military magazine!" Dr. Mabel Harris crowed.

Over an hour was spent taking measurements and photographs of the relic. It was finally time to take a look inside the hull to search for any earthly remains of the two sailors who, at one time in a violent and remote world war, had commandeered this instrument of destruction on behalf of the Japanese Imperial Navy. As large, gaping, rusty holes permeated what was left of the hull, the hold of the vessel could be readily scrutinized.

"No sign of life, or death, for that matter," Professor Harris shouted out to the relief of her compatriots as she scanned the inside of the hull upon her hands and knees with the aid of a bright flashlight.

"Wait!" Mabel Harris warned. "Wait just one moment! Everybody needs to back off right about now! There's live ordnance at the bow of the submarine. It's a Type 95, WWII Japanese torpedo. During its operative hey-day, it had a range of about 10,000 meters, a top speed of around fifty knots, and over 1,200 pounds of TNT compacted within the confines of its warhead. Let me repeat that. I'm talking about 550 kilograms of high explosives, boys and girls! Hands down, to this very day, the Japanese Type 95 is still considered to be the finest torpedo used by any of the combatants during WWII."

"Are we in danger?" Agent McClellan asked.

"Why, yes! We are indeed! With the extensive corrosion involving this particular torpedo that's also compromising the integrity of the warhead and firing mechanism, I venture that it wouldn't take much of a vibration to light up this candle and send us all to kingdom come!"

"This mission is officially over!" McClellan barked. "Gather up your gear and let's cut back through the kiawe grove. I'll whistle out to Skipper Nishioka to bring up the *Poly-Tech Princess* to get us the hell out of here. The two-way isn't working on the cat, so we'll have to motor all the way back to Maalaea to let the Coast Guard know that they'll need to organize a bomb disposal squad to come out here and blow this thing up!"

"Hold on!" Tricia Portal protested. "Why would we have to destroy what's left this historical treasure?"

"It would likely be too dangerous to try and extract the torpedo to diffuse it properly otherwise," Mabel Harris interjected.

"What about the 'October Surprise' that I was hoping to host on national television to bolster-up the George H.W. Bush re-election campaign?"

"The 'Bush-master' should just give a televised hum-job to that horny toad named Bill Clinton and be done with it," Ali'i replied. "That would be a real 'October Surprise' for the deep-state wankers who are entrenched in *both* corrupt political parties, if you were to ask me. Now, Ms. Portal, that would be a T.V. show that one could *really* wrap their lips around, would it not?"

"Hardee-har-har!" Tricia Portal laughed sarcastically, but with a decidedly disappointed pout.

"Let's get the hell out of here," Jeb McClellan said as he pointed to the morass of evil thorns awaiting the expedition team members just beyond the kiawe tree line. "We need to bail out big time before the fucking little Menehune decide to show back up and take us all out for a tasty Sunday morning brunch, if you catch my meaning!"

After the team had returned through the kiawe grove, they made it to the top of the fifteen foot ridge to where they expected to see the *Poly-Tech Princess* anchored off shore. However, it was self-evident that something was dreadfully wrong.

"Agent McClellan!" Dr. Mable Harris said in a panic. "Break out your binoculars! The Princess was anchored just past the breakers and now it's three hundred yards out and drifting toward the South, away from Maui. Something bad happened!"

McClellan gave a play-by-play update. "Anchor line's been cut and the rope tail is dragging upon the water surface. The vessel is adrift and not under power. It's listing about ten degrees, and the cat's railing on the port side is munged-up. Yeah. I agree, Mabel. Something bad happened for sure!"

"Any sign of the skipper?" Ali'i asked. "Maybe he's hurt and below deck."

"Only one way to find out." Jeb McClellan pulled out the referee's whistle from his pocket and gave it to Professor Ali'i. "You blow this thing. Blow it hard, and I'll keep an eye on the catamaran through the binoculars."

Grover Ali'i blew the whistle with all the force that he could rapidly expel from his lungs. There was no response.

"Do it again!" Tricia Portal pleaded. That suggestion turned out to be a terrible idea. The sound of the whistle would turn out to be nothing less than a "come 'n get it" dinner bell for the Menehune who were loitering just north of the Piilani!

"We have to assume that the skipper is either incapacitated or dead," McClellan said. "We only have one viable course of action at this point in time, and that's to head back over to the Saint Isaac's Church Road and hike out. That dirt road might be washed out and impassable in some sections, but I'm confident it'll nonetheless eventually intersect the Piilani. It will be a rather arduous hike, but I'm certain that somebody will likely pick us up once we get to the highway, even though it's sparsely travelled upon nowadays after Hurricane Iniki came by last month."

"Potable water will be an issue," Professor Ali'i said, "as we only brought enough fluid to consume for a day trip, and not more."

"In light of our current circumstances, I think that drinking water will be the least of our concerns," Tricia Portal calmly stated when the team was suddenly surrounded by twenty or more hostile, dark, naked, spear-toting warriors of remarkably short stature.

The explorers were now prisoners of war. They were quickly tethered together with a long leather strap and frog-marched back toward the dry river bed. Before passing back into the kiawe grove, Professor Ali'i took one last look over his shoulder to capture a final glance at the *Poly-Tech Princess,* now peacefully bobbing along the ocean surface about a quarter of a mile from shore.

One of the warriors poked Ali'i in his flank to get his attention. When Ali'i turned to see what was awry, the tribesman pointed his index finger toward the ocean directly at the *Princess* catamaran and said, "Nee-pan! Nee-pan," before offering a malicious grin and rubbing his own peri-gastric abdominal region as if he was reminiscing about a recent, satiating meal. Needless to say, Professor Ali'i was now rather alarmed, as it was a distinct possibility that he and his colleagues would soon be on the menu!

The Menehune and their prisoners hiked up the Waikono river bed and eventually crossed the Piilani Highway unseen, by taking the culvert underpass beneath the road way. The old river bed became narrow the farther up the leeward side of the Haleakala volcano that the prisoners were forced to march. At about an elevation of 2,800 feet the steep path opened into a small, cool, lush plateau where the harsh scrub had given way to a sub-alpine conifer cluster, amongst which a village of about ninety or so Menehune dwelled.

"What do you think of the situation, Dr. Ali'i?" Jeb McClellan whispered.

"This appears to be a self-sustaining paleo-lithic tribe with a population just large enough to prevent genetic mishaps from the inbreeding reproductive events that no doubt must occur within the confines of this isolated village from time to time," Ali'i answered.

"What?! Who gives a shit about these dwarf savages and whether or not they're predisposed to fuck their own mothers just before howling at a full-moon in a collective, post-copulatory rapture?" Tricia Portal asked with a markedly annoyed resonance. "I swear to God, you're an idiot, Professor! The G-man was asking you about *our* fate, not *theirs!*"

"Oh, sorry," the professor sheepishly replied. "As for us, that remains to be seen."

A man who appeared to be a tribal elder was brought forth by several warriors who appeared to act in the capacity as this important individual's bodyguards. Of what could be seen of the other members of the entire village, he was the only person wearing anything at all, and it happened to be a large conch shell propped upon his noodle, as if it were an ancient helmet befitting a Roman Legionnaire.

The elderly individual carefully scrutinized each of the prisoners, first stopping in front of Professor Mabel Harris. The old man smiled and gave a shallow bow at the waist before pointing to the woman and shouting, "Menehune! Menehune."

By expressing a collective high-pitched "whoop", the villagers seemed to be extremely pleased, as if they approved of the presence of this particular prisoner. Except for Mabel's reddish coif and considerably taller stature, she no doubt appeared to look similar to them with dark skin, broad facial features, and nappy hair.

The tribal chieftain mumbled an unintelligible set of instructions to his body guards. They approached Mabel Harris with a sharp, hand crafted knife, and they proceeded to cut her free from the leather straps that held her bound as a prisoner.

Their other captives however, were not treated in such a cordial fashion. When the elder chieftain stopped in front of Professor Ali'i, he turned toward his loyal followers with a scowl upon his face. He pointed back toward the professor and cried out, "Hee Tee! Hee Tee." The crowd became so agitated, it appeared as if a riot was about to ensue. When the chieftain stabbed the ground with the tip of his spear, the screams of rage quickly diminished to little more than an angry, dull roar.

It was now time for the elder to examine the two Caucasians in his royal presence. The chieftain first fondled the blonde hair of Tricia Portal before reaching up and touching the forehead of Special Agent, Jeb McClellan. The elder then turned toward the villagers with a toothless smile and called out, "Roosk! Roosk."

Collectively, the crowd rubbed their abdomens and made a happy sound, indistinguishable from the soft, enthusiastic, melodic hum that a small child would make after a much-anticipated batch of fresh, warm, and soft chocolate chip cookies had just come out of the oven from mom's kitchen!

"Except for Mabel Harris who phenotypically looks like a taller version of these Menehune people," Professor Ali'i said to his colleagues, "the rest of us have been correctly categorized by our racial and ethnic lineage. These people aren't stupid, I tell you!"

"Please explain," Tricia whispered.

"I've got it all figured out," the professor elaborated. "When we were first captured, one of the warriors intimated that he had killed and eaten our skipper, Norman Nishioka. Norman was of Japanese ancestry, just as the sailors who manned the WWII midget submarine that we discovered on the Waikono dry river bed. I'm certain now of the ghastly terminal fate of those two Japanese submariners. They were no doubt captured and eventually eaten. I'm certain before they died, the sailors tried to explain to the Menehune that they were from 'Japan'. Phonetically, 'Nihon', and eventually the term was linguistically bastardized by the tribe to the name that they called the skipper–'Nee-pan'. Get it?"

"Well, you don't know for certain that the skipper's dead. What about you specifically, professor?" Tricia asked.

"I suspect through long oral tradition, they are very much aware that their people had engaged in lethal warfare against the Polynesians eons ago. Polynesians from Tahiti, to be precise. The tribal chieftain called me, 'Hee-Tee'. That can't be a coincidence. As for you, the elder referred to you and Agent McClellan as 'Roosk'. Russian. Phonetically, 'Russkiy' and eventually linguistically truncated by the tribe to the name, 'Roosk', which is actually quite appropriate."

"How so?" the FBI agent asked for clarity.

"Look, McClellan," Ali'i explained, "you and the lost Russian colonists from almost two centuries ago are, or were, all Caucasian! Caucus Mountains. Russian. Russkiy. Roosk. Get it?"

"Do you still have your government issued, 1911, .45 caliber side arm?" Mabel Harris asked.

"I do indeed." the G-man replied. "Right here in my holster. It wasn't confiscated by our captors, as obviously, they'd never seen a semi-automatic pistol before. I only have one full magazine and the weapon is loaded. If push comes to shove, I'll use that pistol on all of us first before I'll allow the Menehune to eat us while we're still very much alive. Did you receive any side-arm training while you were in the Navy a while back, Dr. Harris?"

"I did," Dr. Harris answered, "but I've got two more important commodities under my sleeve that may prove to give us all a distinct tactical advantage, if and when things around here get a little dicey."

"What would that be?" The agent asked.

"I'm *urban* and I'm *black*," Dr. Harris said with a hearty laugh in the face of death, just before giving Agent McClellan a most-welcome peck on his cheek. "Nothing else you need to know, white boy!"

The tribal elder went over to a pile of neatly stacked human remains in the center of the village and reached into a collection of what appeared to be human long bones comprised of lower extremity femurs and upper extremity humeri. The chieftain extracted an ancient coin and brought it back to Jeb McClellan for him to evaluate.

"Roosk! Roosk." the chief said.

"What is it? Tricia asked.

"Wow!" Jeb answered. "It's an old, Catherine the Great, five Kopek coin minted in 1796! This must have still been in circulation amongst the Russian colonists who disappeared in the early 1800s!"

"Can't you see?" Ali'i asked. "The chief just offered you a gift! These people aren't evil! I just don't see any evidence to verify the mistaken impression that you may have of them as of yet, Jeb. They're just scared of us! Nothing more, and nothing less..."

Sadly, the professor thought the coin handed to Jeb McClellan was a gracious token of respect. Sadly, nothing could have been further from the truth at that juncture. The coin would soon turn out to be part of a sacrificial ritual, heretofore unbeknownst by the anthropologist.

"Well, I'm still not so sure about that," McClellan said as he smiled, bowed, and handed the coin back to the chief. The chief snatched the coin, kissed it, and smiled yet again before he thrust his spear deep into the abdomen of the now-doomed FBI agent!

As the G-man fell, the chief's bodyguards swarmed Jeb McClellan who was unable to extract his weapon from its holster. As he was repeatedly stabbed, the Special Agent glared up at Grover Ali'i before muttering his last words. "If you ever saw a victim dying in agony with a spear thrust into his breadbasket, would that be enough evidence for you, Professor?"

While professor Ali'i and Tricia Portal briefly stood frozen in terror, the former naval lieutenant, Professor Mabel Harris, jumped into action. She calmly extracted the dead agent's side arm from its holster, chambered a round, and then placed the barrel of the weapon directly against the forehead of the tribal chief.

"Menehune!" the elder said as he closed his eyes before reaching out in an attempt to embrace the woman he erroneously believed to be a taller member of his own race. The chieftain, nor any of his tribal members, had any idea that Mabel Harris was now in possession of the late Jeb McClellan's deadly weapon!

"Menehune!" the Chief repeated.

"Menehune, my ass!" Mabel Harris said. "Let me see if that stupid conch shell that's propped upon your microcephalic noggin can possibly stop a hot, smokin' round from this 1911 edition Colt Combat Commander forty-five caliber hand cannon."

With that, Mabel pulled the trigger and violently separated the head of the tribal elder from the thick, bull-neck to which it was previously attached!

"Nope," Mabel Harris said. "It would appear to me that your crappy, conch-shell helmet would most likely fail the current United

States Occupational, Safety, and Health Administration Guidelines for adequate, on-the-job, protective head gear."

The villagers hit the ground and covered their heads with their hands in terror. This was now an opportunity for Professor Ali'i and Tricia Portal to make a hasty retreat.

"Run!" Mabel ordered her colleagues. "I'll hold them off as long as I can. Get out of here, now!"

"Wait! What about you?" Tricia asked.

"Run!" This was Mabel's only reply.

As professor Ali'i and Tricia Portal fled out of the village at neck-break speed, they heard a memorable snippet of a sardonic soliloquy that emanated from the lips of their now-doomed colleague—a colleague who had somehow instantaneously transformed into a brave and selfless hero.

"Times being what they are, I guess I'll declare myself to be the chief cook and bottle washer of this shit-show," Mabel Harris proclaimed to her new, albeit short-lived, subjugated tribal members. "You nasty little circus freaks are now going to be working for me, and I better not hear any complaints about the new management that has just initiated what I'd describe to be nothing more than a hostile corporate take-over. I'm your new queen, do you understand? Somebody better get me some fresh, sliced, tropical fruit and a refreshing, ice-cold beer. If I'm going to die today, which will likely be the case, then one of you little monkey-fuckers needs to come over here, kneel down in front of me, and give me a top-shelf muff-munch until I scream like a rabid banshee suddenly enveloped in the multiple, repetitive and rhythmic tsunamic waves of orgasmic ecstasy!"

That was the last thing Mabel Harris said that Ali'i and Trish Portal could fully discern as they fled the village. "Let's climb to the summit of Haleakala" Tricia Portal said. "There's a trail that circumnavigates the crater with people walking upon it all the time. There's a ranger station up there, also. We'll be able to find help up there!"

"That's more than a seven thousand foot vertical climb from where we now stand. I'm not exactly a young man any more. We'll never make it! We've got to stay together, but we've got to go downhill. We've got to go downhill right now!" The professor explained. The duo booked down the hillside as fast as they could, using the natural path of the Waikono dry river bed as their trail. On two occasions, Professor Ali'i stumbled on the river rocks and fell, but fortunately when this occurred, he was able to immediately bounce back up and continue his rapid, downward trek toward the ocean.

After several minutes, the unmistakable repetitive sound of gun fire in the distance could be heard, echoing down the canyon river bed. "How many shots did you count?" the professor asked.

"Five," Tricia said. "If you include the first round Mabel used to kill the tribal chief, that makes a total of six shots thus far."

"Shit!" The professor exclaimed. "That means she only has one round left. I hope she saves it for herself!" No sooner had those words passed through professor's vocal cords, the final round that Professor Mabel Harris had at her disposal was subsequently discharged.

"They'll be coming for us now!" Tricia said. "Keep running!" Within an hour, the duo had reached the Piilani Highway.

"We're saved!" The Professor cheered. "I'm exhausted. Let's just wait here and surely a car will come by here soon enough that will be able to render assistance."

After twenty or so minutes, a pickup truck finally pulled over to the side of the road to give the remnants of the expeditionary team a much-needed lift back to civilization. Just as Tricia and Professor Ali'i were climbing into the back bed of the pickup truck however, a spear was hurled at the vehicle that slammed into the windshield, cracking the glass. Fearing that he was being set up for a robbery or car-jacking attempt, the driver of the truck floored the accelerator and sped away in a shroud of grit and dust, causing the professor and his companion to tumble out the back of the truck and onto the dirt road.

A solitary Menehune lead scout was upon the professor and Tricia Portal in no time. A thrust from the spear of the warrior punctured the right lung of the professor. Grover Ali'i began to gasp and sputter before he expectorated copious amounts of bright red blood from his now critically injured pulmonary tree.

The scout was about to inflict a lethal laceration upon the anterior throat of the recumbent professor, but fortunately, the ever-resourceful Tricia Portal leapt into the breach. Extracting the spiked kiawe branch hidden in her backpack, she clutched her make-shift weapon much as a seasoned sommelier would grasp a corkscrew in a dusty basement wine cellar hidden beneath the floorboards of a snooty, upscale, Texas steak house.

With all her might, she plunged the four inch, iron-hard kiawe thorn into the face of the assailant, puncturing his left eyeball before the spike passed through the relatively thin, bony posterior wall of the scout's retro-ocular orbit. As the toxic barb penetrated deep into the scout's brain, he stumbled and fell away to the side before suffering a grand mal seizure. Afterward, the warrior simply quit breathing altogether!

"Nice! Nicely done," Ali'i stuttered. "We better keep moving. There'll be more like him coming our way."

"Wait! You're badly hurt!" Tricia protested.

"It's just a flesh wound, Sarge!" The professor exclaimed with a sarcastic half-grin, as he tried to channel his inner John Wayne, straight from the screenplay of the Duke's starring role in the Sands of Iwo Jima. "Just get me back to the two-manned Japanese submarine. I know what needs to be done."

By the time the duo had reached the WWII relic, Professor Ali'i was spent as he'd already lost nearly half of his blood volume. The voluminous hemorrhage from his open chest wound left a long trail that was easy for the Menehune warriors to follow along the path of the rocky, dry river bed.

"I can't go any further, but I've got a big surprise for these nasty sons-of-bitches. You need to head out into the ocean and swim to the *Poly-Tech Princess*. If you can't find the key in the ignition switch, don't worry. The Research Institute always makes sure there's an extra key on board in the glove box at the helm. If you make it back home Tricia, tell everybody that the anthropological opinions I espoused on this ill-fated expedition were all wrong," Professor Ali'i gasped while attempting to express his last measure of intellectual honesty. "In fact, I was dead wrong about *everything*!"

"What do you mean, Professor?"

"The Menehune are *not* extinct. They're indeed still out there," Professor Ali'i said. "Without doubt, as there's not any better description that comes to my now oxygen-starved and actively dying brain cells, they're ruthless and evil beyond measure. Now, go!"

The professor patiently watched as Ms. Portal disappeared down the river bed to enter the ocean. Once she was out of sight, with what little respiratory reserve he could possibly muster, Professor Ali'i began to blow upon the referee whistle to beckon the trailing warriors toward him.

Momentarily, twenty or more Menehune were sprinting down the dry river bed directly at the remnants of the rusty, miniature Japanese submarine. When his adversaries were well within only a thirty yard distance, the professor crawled through a gaping hole in the hull toward the bow of the ship and he positioned himself upon the solitary torpedo that was still on the vessel.

Ali'i found a rusty wrench on the sub, and he used it to hammer away at the firing cap nipple that extruded from the end of the warhead. Nothing happened! After the third strike upon the head of the firing cap, the Menehune warriors had already breached the hull and they were clawing away at the professor who was now within their reach!

The professor finally realized that there was a safety mechanism on the fulminated mercury firing cap nipple. It was a simple cotter pin that prevented the firing cap from igniting the warhead until the torpedo was ready to be fired from the bow tube. The safety pin was so rusty, that Professor Ali'i was able to simply snap it away with his thumb and index finger. Once done, the next strike against the firing cap nipple did the trick.

The explosion of the 550 kilogram warhead on the Japanese Type 95 torpedo turned what little remained of the WWII submarine into an enormous plume of rusty shrapnel fragments and oxidized dust, while completely vaporizing the professor and nearly two dozen of the Menehune warriors.

Although Tricia Portal was already a hundred yards out into the ocean, the blast was deafening. "Thank you professor Grover Ali'i. You saved my life. Thank you, Professor Mabel Harris. You also saved my life. I'll never forget either of you!"

Slow and steady wins the race, Tricia thought. The *Poly-Tech Princess* was now a mile offshore. Although it would be a difficult and exhausting swim, she had no doubt in her mind that she would make it. After all, on intermittent occasions in San Francisco, crazy contestants eagerly compete in a two mile swim out to Alcatraz in fifty degree water!

As long as Tricia didn't get eaten by a tiger shark, or on the other hand, get stung with a lethal dose of invertebrate neurotoxin from an innocuous appearing box jellyfish that just happened to be blithely floating by, she'd likely make it. After all, she would never have any better physique in her entire life than what physical condition she was in at that very moment.

When Tricia Portal finally arrived to the swim platform affixed to the stern of the *Poly-Tech Princess*, she was thoroughly exhausted. She had to gather considerable energy before she could even possibly climb up the three-step rung that led up to the rear deck of the catamaran.

While she sat on the swim platform and dangled her legs into the water to catch her breath, she heard stirring down in the hold of the vessel. "Skipper, is that you?" There was no answer.

"Skipper Nishioka?" She called out one more time before she turned to look over her shoulder to see who was approaching her from behind. Unbeknownst to Tricia Portal, the Skipper was now long dead and gone. Sadly, the *Poly-Tech Princess* was currently occupied by an uninvited boarding party of ravenous savages who had absolutely no intention of ever allowing the young woman to return home...

Without the benefit of an "October Surprise", George H.W. Bush lost in his second presidential bid just a few weeks later to a sleazy, sexual satyr named, William Jefferson Clinton from Hope, Arkansas on November 2, 1982.

On the following day, the Coast Guard finally released its official report concerning the ill-fated voyage of the *Poly-Tech Princess* mishap from the month before. When the catamaran had been hauled back into the Maalaea Harbor by a tender boat from *La Paloma Del Pacifico*, there was no sign of life on the abandoned boat. The Coast Guard forensic team had crawled all over the vessel and did not find any hard evidence of foul play, except for the miscellaneous and non-specific broken railing involving the port side of the craft. That was indeed an oddity that would sadly remain forever unanswered.

"Tell me, Captain Lewis," the Coast Guard Commander asked his subordinate, "are you now ready, once and for all, to put your report to bed concerning this most unfortunate matter regarding the mysterious fate of the crew of the *Poly-Tech Princess*?"

"I've finally got it all tied together, Commander," Captain Lewis answered.

"I certainly hope so," the Commander added, "as we've got a lot more work ahead of us if we're ever going to hunt down those damned Chi-coms who are continuing to smuggle narcotics into the islands."

"Frankly, it was a bit of a rush job, and a few of the corners might have been trimmed a bit close if you catch my meaning," the Captain replied, "but nonetheless, I am indeed ready to officially wrap this up with my final signature, Sir."

"Well," the Commander pressed, "what's your final verdict?"

"A rogue wave must have cleared the deck and washed the entire crew overboard," Captain Lewis answered. "Everybody likely drowned. A reasonable conclusion, no doubt, at least from the final forensic assessment. However, it's a big bad, Pacific, as you well know, Commander. If the crew didn't drown, there's a distinct possibility that they might have actually been *eaten alive by something or other*."

"What do you make of the two Catherine the Great 5 kopec Russian coins that were found on board? As I was told, they were left by somebody upon the chart table near the marine head," the Commander wondered as he pressed for a rational explanation. "They dated all the way back to the late 1700s, did they not?"

"I have no idea," Captain Lewis answered. "None of the living relatives of any of the individuals who were apparently lost at sea have expressed any knowledge about these rare and valuable Russian artifacts. I guess the two coins will simply end up in a box of other unclaimed items in a dark and dank evidence locker somewhere. There's nothing else to say, Commander. The case is now officially closed..."

THE END